THE BEAR'S CLAWS

THE PARANORMAL COUNCIL #6

LAURA GREENWOOD

BLURB

Can they heal each others wounds, or will they live the rest of their lives alone?

The only way for Vic to deal with the death of his parents, is to hide away in the woods, doing everything that he can to avoid his responsibilities as the panther alpha.

For years, Nita believed that her entire family was dead. But hearing a rumour that her cousin is still alive, she sets out to find him.

A chance encounter in the woods, brings the two shifters together, and something quickly sparks between them.

CHAPTER ONE

NITA WASN'T one to panic. She'd been on her own too long for that. And yet, panicked was how she felt right at that moment in time. She couldn't help it, not with the odd sensation of being watched that had accompanied her since she'd first entered the forest three days ago.

It wasn't that she was particularly worried about what could happen to her. No matter what, she'd survived worse in her life, and she had her secret to protect her. After all, no one ever expected the unassuming dark-haired girl to be able to turn into a wild animal. In hindsight, it might have been safer for her to travel in bear form from the start, but then bears were a rarity in these parts. Plus, she tried not to shift unless absolutely necessary. Not after what happened to her family.

Nita shivered, the cold air and the memories making her uncomfortable. Well, the memories mostly. Being a shifter meant that she didn't feel the cold too much, even if she was only wearing a thin t-shirt and worn jeans.

The forest was beginning to darken, taking on a gloomy tinge and making her consider whether she was going to carry on in the dark or make camp for the evening. Part of her felt that the first option was far better, seeing in the dark wasn't a problem for her, but the other part of her was saying she needed rest.

She couldn't very well turn up at her long-lost cousin's home tired and grungy. She had enough going against her as it was. Like the fact that they'd never actually met before, and that they'd both believed that their entire family was dead up until a few weeks ago. Though Nita supposed that he still thought that. She'd only learnt about her cousin from an old letter of her grandfather's she'd found.

And so, she'd started her journey, with only her own wits and determination to guide her. She'd had nothing in Russia, no real home, no family, no money. Nothing. Not even a boyfriend, though that wasn't surprising given that she had so little to offer someone. And that most shifters still believed that they had a true mate out there somewhere. Nita was no different, though for her it was more of a hope that there was.

She briefly wondered whether her cousin had found his mate, and if she'd be nice to Nita or not. Or maybe her cousin's mate was a he, it wasn't unheard of, and while she didn't know what two male shifter mates would do about having cubs, it was widely accepted within society. Not that she'd ever truly been part of shifter culture. She'd been on the fringes for years, yet another reason for leaving Russia as soon as she could.

She gave in to the need for rest, especially as she could smell a river nearby. Not only would she be able to stop for the night, but she'd be able to get clean for the first time in days. Maybe, if she was really lucky, she would be able to catch a fish to cook. She knew it was slightly stereotypical for a bear to like fish, but she couldn't help it. Just thinking about freshly cooked salmon, with a dill sauce or covered in chilli flakes, was making her mouth water. It'd been too long since she'd had a decent meal.

Having found a good tree to use to build her den for the night, Nita searched around for the kind of sticks and leaves she'd need. Luckily, it was still spring, and there was plenty to choose from. Not so luckily, it felt like it might rain, though she supposed that she was planning on taking a dip in the river anyway, so it might not matter so much.

She stepped back to admire her handiwork, feeling twin pangs of sadness and pride. It'd been her Dad that had taught her to do this kind of thing, and while she remembered those days with fondness, it often came with the grief that hadn't lessened much over the intervening years. Though she supposed she at least hadn't let a need for vengeance take over, even if she had been angry when she'd learned of her family's deaths. But, once she was settled and properly on her feet for the first time in her life, she was going to see what she could do about combatting poachers in general. She was sure that she wasn't the only shifter whose family had been stolen by them, and that was without the risk that their animal counterparts had to endure.

Nita walked the little way to the river, surprised to find that it was closer than she'd first thought. Trying to ignore the sensation of being watched, which had never really gone away, she peeled off her clothes, dunking them straight in the water and scrubbing them with the small cake of soap that she'd brought with her. It wouldn't have the same results as a washing machine would, but at least they'd be clean. She wrung them out and hung them over a low hanging branch. They weren't likely to dry much in the slightly chilly spring air, but once she got a fire going they would.

Bracing herself for the cold, Nita walked slowly into the river. Despite the fact that the sun had been shining all day, and that she didn't feel the cold as much as a human would, the cold water caused goosebumps up and down her body. She ducked her head under the water, and attempted to scrub her hair the best she could. It might be particularly vain of her, but she liked having clean hair, even while she was trekking through the forest with no one to see her.

Except that wasn't quite true. The moment she broke free of the water, it felt like she was being watched.

CHAPTER TWO

THERE WAS someone in his forest. He'd smelt the other predator a few days ago, and had relentlessly tracked them ever since, trying to work out what they were doing in his territory. But so far, he'd come up with nothing. And whatever it was, it seemed to do a decent job of hiding. Which is what had convinced Vic that it was another shifter he was dealing with and not another animal.

He was the panther alpha, even if he hadn't done anything about that since his parents had died. He assumed that his brother, Kem, had been keeping things going in his absence. That was just the kind of person Kem was. Vic felt a slight pang of guilt about abandoning his younger brother, but he pushed it to the side. He wasn't in any fit state to be an alpha right now, and guilt wasn't going to change that.

He pushed open the leaves of the tree he was perched in. He'd climbed up in panther form but shifted back so he could use his hands. His eyes locked on to the lone figure who appeared to be bathing in the river, and he nearly fell out of the tree in shock; that was not what he'd been expecting. Or rather, she wasn't what he'd been expecting.

The smell, and the other signs of an intruder he'd seen, had suggested that it was something much bigger he was tracking, possibly even a bear. Yet the woman in front of him was slight, with long dark hair. The only way he even knew she wasn't a child was because of the size of her chest.

Even if he knew he should, Vic couldn't tear his eyes away. She wasn't even doing anything particularly exciting, other than washing herself, and while she was naked, Vic had become desensitised to that; as was to be expected with shifters. For the first time in years, Vic found himself wondering what it would feel like to have a woman under him, her soft moans and whimpers in his ears.

A loud splash sounded, breaking him out of his fantasies, and he looked to find the woman stood at the edge of the river, hands on her hips and looking right at him.

"I know you're there, stop hiding you coward," she shouted in his direction. Vic just sat there in silence, not quite knowing what to do. The woman started tapping her foot impatiently, as if she'd had to do this a thousand times before.

Vice sighed, and pictured his panther form, shifting effortlessly. In one graceful leap, he jumped down from the tree, and stalked towards the woman on the ground. She couldn't see him yet, but when she did, he fully expected her to run away screaming, not used to a big cat walking towards her. Except that wasn't quite right; if she was a shifter, it wasn't likely to phase her at all. But that didn't stop him.

He slinked into the clearing, and stood opposite the woman, taking her in with his glowing yellow eyes. She was even more attractive close-up, and if he'd been in human form, he was sure he wouldn't have been able to hide what he thought.

"I know you're a shifter," she said, speaking more softly this time, with a slight hint of an accent, though Vic had no idea what kind. Her hands were still on her hips, and he liked how the position pushed up her breasts. The alpha in him *definitely* liked that. As did the man. He cocked his head to the side, and she sighed. A sure sign that he wasn't going to get anywhere while still in animal form. Knowing he might regret it, he pictured himself as a human again, and transformed before her.

The woman's brown eyes took him in, travelling

very slowly over his body. Vic stood there, waiting for her to finish. He knew he looked good, he had to after years of living in the forest and doing everything for himself. His muscles had become more defined, especially as it was easier for shifters to gain them too. Her gaze lingered between his legs, making Vic smirk. Least he knew he still had that effect on women.

"What are you doing here?" he asked, his voice feeling slightly gravelly from not using it much. The woman looked up sharply, and managed to keep her eyes on his face this time. He hadn't noticed how tall she was from the tree, but probably because he'd been focusing on her other attributes at the time.

"Travelling." He frowned, not liking the one-word answer.

"Through my forest?" he threw at her. A low growl rumbling in his throat. She cocked an eyebrow, as if to say she wasn't impressed.

"I don't think the forest belongs to anyone," she answered calmly.

"It does now."

"Look," she said sternly, "I'm not looking to move into your territory or anything. I'm just travelling through on my way to see my cousin."

"There are faster ways to travel," he responded tersely.

"And if I could afford them, then I would be using them," she snapped, anger flaring in her eyes. "Look, I don't want any trouble. Why don't you come back to my camp with me, and I'll share some of the fish I caught with you." She waved her hand towards a small pile of fish that she must have caught while in the river.

"Okay," Vic answered, against his better judgement. He didn't know what had made him say it, other than the fact that this woman was making him feel more than he had in years, and if he could preserve that, then he would.

CHAPTER THREE

Nɪᴛᴀ sᴛᴏᴋᴇᴅ ᴛʜᴇ ꜰɪʀᴇ, trying not to let her eyes stray to the man at the other side of it. He was broad, with dark features and a brooding stare that seemed to hold more pain than she'd ever seen, even when she looked in the mirror. He was also completely naked, something she was trying to avoid thinking about. Nita herself had put on a long t-shirt, feeling oddly under, and over, dressed at the same time. While she was a shifter, and used to being naked around others, it felt different because of how physically attracted to him she was. Thankfully, it was probably nothing more than her need for sex that had her feeling like this; it'd been a while since she'd had any, and her inner bear was making itself known as a consequence.

"So, your cousin?" the man asked, shifting

nervously on the log he was sitting on. Nita got the impression that he didn't spend much time around other people. And not just because he'd referred to the forest as his.

"Yes, he lives in the city I think." She turned over the skewer of fish so that it didn't burn.

"Will I know him?" the man asked, and Nita looked up sharply. "I didn't always live in the woods," he added after seeing her expression.

"I only know he lives there and the family name he has. I didn't even realise he was alive until a couple of weeks ago," she admitted, not quite sure why she felt comfortable telling him that.

"Oh?" Nita sighed.

"Our name is Hendricks," she told him, and his face screwed up in a look of concentration.

"The name sounds vaguely familiar," he mused. The two of them sat in silence, listening to the sizzle of the fire as it cooked the fish. "Will you tell me your first name?"

"Nita," she answered, finding it odd that the two of them had got this far without actually introducing themselves. But it had been so long since she'd been an active part of normal life that she'd forgotten about social niceties.

"I'm Vic, it's, er, nice to meet you," he said, sounding even less certain than she did.

"What brings you to the woods, Vic?" She smirked at him, but had secretly enjoyed the way his name sounded as she said it. She wondered if it was short for something, but she didn't want to ask. She hated her full name, and wouldn't want a virtual stranger asking about it. Vic looked undecided, as if he didn't know how he wanted to answer. Nita waited patiently, it wasn't like she had anywhere else to be.

"My parents died." He looked down as sadness filled his eyes. Nita felt guilty about pushing him, but if he hadn't actually wanted to tell her, then she suspected he wouldn't have.

"I'm sorry." Her thoughts went to her own parents, who she'd lost to poachers near the Russian border. It'd been a hard few years after it had happened, but at least she could remember them without completely breaking down now.

"Thank you," he whispered. "I've never actually said that out loud before." His eyes appeared pained, though he wasn't about to cry at least.

On impulse, Nita stood up and walked to his side of the fire, sitting down beside him, she placed one of her hands on top of his clenched fists. With the change of conversation, she'd even managed to push the thoughts of him being naked to the back of her mind.

"Want to talk about it now?" she asked, carefully keeping her voice soft. A pang of sadness travelled through her as she thought of her grandfather talking to her like this when she'd been a little girl. No matter how trivial her upset had been, he'd always listened. She'd gone to him with everything, from grazed knees, to the time that her high school boyfriend broke her heart.

Vic looked up, conflicted feelings clear in his deep green eyes. She imagined that he felt a little bit like she did right now; wary of being around a stranger, but trusting them all the same. It was an odd feeling, but with Vic sat next to her, she felt safer and more secure than she had in weeks. Possibly even years.

"It was a car crash, of all things. One day, they were having dinner with me and my younger brother. The next, they were gone." She rubbed her thumb over the back of his hand as he spoke, understanding just how he felt.

"I'm sorry," she said again, not knowing what to say. While she guessed she could tell him about her own loss, she didn't want to cheapen what he was feeling.

"It was years ago," he said, sounding wistful. "I should be over it."

"It's not an easy thing to get over. Not when they

were the people who raised you. Taught you how to hunt and fend for yourself," she said. Surprisingly, Vic laughed.

"That's such a shifter thing to say." She smiled at his response, allowing him to change the subject. She didn't really have any right to push further.

"There's no escaping that upbringing," she responded.

Vic turned his face to hers, and she hadn't realised quite how close the two of them had been sitting. Her eyes flitted down to his slightly parted lips, and before she knew it, he'd pressed them against hers.

It took her a moment to respond, but once she did, she deepened the kiss, feeling something long dead wake up inside her. She'd been with men before, but their kisses had never been anything like this. Vic's hand cupped her cheek, the gentle pressure of it only adding to her enjoyment.

Almost as suddenly as it had started, he broke the kiss, and stared at her in shock. Vic jumped to his feet, shifted and ran off into the night. Leaving Nita unsure about what had just happened. But if he thought she'd forget a kiss like that, then he had another thing coming.

CHAPTER FOUR

VIC SHIFTED AS HE RAN, four powerful legs replacing his own; hopefully, his dark coat would help him blend into the forest and not be easily seen by Nita. He knew that it wasn't particularly fair of him to run away, especially after the kiss they'd just shared.

And what a kiss. Which was the whole problem. Since his parents' deaths, he'd tried to avoid feeling anything at all, and he'd become pretty good at it too. One kiss with a pretty shifter had been all it took to undo all that hard work though. He could feel the emotions welling up inside him and threatening to overflow. He wasn't sure what it was about her, but what he was feeling reminded him of his brother's voicemails a couple of months ago.

Vic felt bad for not returning Kem's calls now, and for not picking up the phone in the first place.

Yet another reason it was better not to feel anything. He could avoid feeling bad about ignoring his younger brother, and the responsibilities he'd thrust on Kem by disengaging with the world. At least Kem sounded happy on his messages. Or he had in the last few months. From the sound of it, he'd met his mate, and she'd turned his world upside down. She sounded nice, and a part of Vic wanted to meet the woman that had made his little brother so happy. Unfortunately, it was the other part that won out. Vic didn't want to be around people; he just couldn't stand false sympathy.

He came to an abrupt halt when he got back to the clearing that he called his home. There, leaning against his front door in nothing but the long t-shirt she'd been wearing, was Nita. And she was looking at him with a mixture of curiosity and confusion in her eyes.

Vic pictured his human form, and morphed back quicker than she could blink.

"Please, I'm a shifter," she answered before he'd even had time to ask the question. Which a bit disturbing if anyone asked him. But weirdly, he kind of liked that.

"That's one hell of a nose," he muttered. Nita laughed, clearly taking it as the compliment it was.

He could appreciate that in a woman; he didn't have time for the types that were insulted by everything.

"Your scent is all over the woods, Vic. It wasn't difficult," she said, pushing away from the door and stalking towards him with the grace of a predator. Not a big cat like him though, and he wondered if his earlier suspicion of her being a bear shifter was correct.

"What are you?" he asked, curiosity getting the better of him. Normally it was seen as impolite to ask, but this wasn't exactly a normal situation. It wasn't often that women came trekking through the woods on their way to see a long-lost cousin. It almost sounded like a fairy tale. Which he supposed would make him the big bad wolf. Eating her wasn't quite what he had in mind though. Nita's eyes flicked downwards, where clear evidence of the direction of his thoughts.

Instead of berating him, Nita licked her lips slowly, causing Vic's groin to tighten. He hadn't been with a woman since before he'd first come into the woods, and just the sight of her was enough to get him going. Or maybe that was Nita herself. While most shifters had a high sex drive, Vic's had been almost non-existent for the past few years, even before he'd come to the woods.

"I'm a bear. A Kamchatka brown bear to be

precise," she said as she reached him. Slowly, she reached out and stroked his cheek; her touch feather-light, as if she was worried he'd run off again.

"There are different types of bear shifter?" he asked, surprised that it wasn't something he'd already known.

"Why wouldn't there be?" She shrugged, and trailed her hand down until it was resting on his chest. She stepped forward, closing the gap between them, and he could feel the warmth of her body even through the t-shirt. "There are different types of bear after all," she added.

Vic looked down at her, though she wasn't actually much shorter than he was anyway. Instead of answering, he leaned in and kissed her again, pulling her to him further with an arm around her waist. The feel of her body pressed against his was almost more than he could take, and his inner-panther purred when she deepened the kiss. Here was a woman that wasn't afraid of his shifter side. Vic had very little doubt that Nita would take what she wanted, regardless of what anyone else thought.

CHAPTER FIVE

He deepened the kiss, and it was all that Nita could do to stay standing and not wrap her legs around Vic's waist. It'd been too long since she'd been with a man anyway, and adding in his scent was driving her a little bit crazy.

Alright, it was driving her a lot crazy. Giving in to her instincts, and with Vic's help, she jumped up so that her legs were wrapped around him, his hands cupping her ass as he held her to him.

"Nita," he growled as he pulled away from their kiss, his eyes flashing amber. She briefly wondered if he'd spent too much time alone in the woods and his shifter side was dangerously prominent, but she pushed the thought aside. It wasn't like she was defenceless, and her bear form was bigger than his panther; if it came to it, she could protect herself.

To her surprise, Vic carried her towards the doorway she'd been standing in, barely breaking a sweat despite the fact he had two people's weight to move. He quickly unlatched the door, and in mere seconds, she found herself thrown down onto a surprisingly soft double bed.

She looked around her, taking in the clean and simple surroundings. This was clearly a man who didn't feel the need for extravagant surroundings, and she could respect that. It fit right in with her life. She could easily imagine herself slotting into this world, which shocked Nita more than a little bit. She almost never thought of settling down with anyone.

Vic didn't give her a chance to think about it anymore, as he crawled up her body, his broad chest and strong muscles completely distracting her from thoughts of domesticity. In fact, her thoughts now took a rather wicked turn, encouraged by the glint in his eyes.

She craned her head up, so that she could capture his lips with hers and hurry the situation along a bit. Despite the logical side of her thinking that this was a bad idea, especially as she'd only known him for such a short period of time, the rest of her was overriding it. Something about being here with Vic felt more right than she could possibly fathom.

Breaking the kiss, she pushed him onto his back,

grateful that he decided to play along or she'd never have moved him. She straddled him, whipping off the t-shirt she was wearing as she did, leaving both of them completely naked. Beneath her, Vic's breathing hitched, and she smiled in victory. She seemed to be having an effect on him despite the fact he'd already seen her naked. She could live with that.

Leaning down, she nipped Vic's earlobe, causing a rumbling sound to come from his chest, but that only spurred her on more. She kissed his neck, moving across his chest. Running her hand downwards, she took hold of him, stroking him firmly as she continued her journey.

Vic groaned, and Nita revelled in the knowledge that she was causing the reaction. Looking up his body, with a wicked smile on her face, she took him into her mouth. Vic's hands flew to her head, twisting his fingers into her long dark hair. He didn't try to move her, but the pressure only encouraged Nita, and she moved faster.

"Nita," he half-panted, half-growled her name, filling her with pride. "Stop," he pleaded. She lifted her head, and saw a pained expression on his face.

She moved back up his body, and the moment he could, he gave her a searing kiss, which made her feel more alive than anything she'd ever experienced before. His hands moved from her hair, over her body, causing a trail of fire wherever he touched.

He slipped a hand between her legs, and she whimpered as he pushed gently fingers inside her. She already knew that she was ready for him, but the surprise on his face when he noticed too was worth keeping that quiet. Still, Vic didn't stop, and Nita threw her head back in ecstasy, loving what he was doing to her.

She could feel the pleasure building inside her, but wanted to hold off until the right moment. She pulled his hand away, and positioned herself over him, impatient for the main event to begin. Nita guided him into her, and they both groaned as they joined together.

The two of them began moving, setting a frantic pace that was dictated by the connection between them. Mid-thrust, Vic turned them so that Nita was lying on her back, allowing him to drive into her deeper.

Nita felt her teeth lengthening in her mouth, but was too engrossed in the moment to fully under-stand what was happening. Without realising what she was doing, she sunk her teeth into Vic's shoul-der, feeling the tell-tale prick that suggested he'd done the same to her. The moment they did, she exploded, taking her to dizzying new heights.

Vic collapsed on the bed beside her, both of them breathing heavily.

"Wow," she muttered, once she'd regained the power of speech. She'd had sex before, but it had never been like that.

"Mmm," he agreed, throwing an arm over her.

"We bit each other," she said, sitting bolt upright. Vic absentmindedly stroked her back, but it didn't help much.

"Did you not like it?" Vic asked warily.

"Yes, but..."

"But?"

"Doesn't that mean we're mated?" His hand stilled on her back as he considered what she was saying. The thought kept swimming around in Nita's head, along with all the warnings of what happened to shifters who mated accidentally.

"I'm not sure."

"How can you not be sure?" she almost yelled, panic rising inside her. While more than a little part of her wanted Vic again, the thought of them being stuck together if they weren't true mates, was scaring her. Mates were a big deal for shifters, and she didn't want to think that she'd blown it.

Her breathing shallowed as she began to panic and she sensed, rather than saw, Vic move so that he was sat next to her.

"Nita, please breathe slowly. We're fine, we can sort it out."

"How?" she said in a strangled sounding voice, but tried to do as he said. She breathed in, counting to three as she did, before repeating it with her outward breath.

"I'll call my brother, he'll know someone that can sort it out," Vic said. Nita turned to look at him, already feeling a little calmer, and saw the uneasy look on his face.

"You sure?" He nodded once in response.

"Yes."

CHAPTER SIX

THE PHONE CONTINUED TO RING, making the lump in
Vic's throat grow even more. To say he was nervous
was an understatement. He was under no illusions
that he'd been a terrible brother to Kem, and that his
brother had every right to hate him.

"Hello?" a sleepy voice sounded down the phone.

"Kem?" Vic's voice cracked slightly as he said his
brother's name. He hated how stirred up his
emotions were by doing something as simple as
making a phone call. They talked on the phone every
so often, and it always seemed to stir up the same
emotions.

"Vic, is that you?" A rustling sound accompanied
Kem's question, almost like he was sitting up in bed;
much like Vic himself was. Nita pressed a trail of
kisses across his shoulder blades, soothing his raging

emotions and giving him more confidence than he'd had before.

"Yes, I'm sorry," Vic said, knowing that it wasn't nearly enough to make up for abandoning him after their parents died. Especially given that Kem had also been required to take on Vic's responsibilities as the panther shifter alpha. While panthers were solitary by nature, they did need at least some guidance. Particularly with the growing focus on politics that seemed to be a thing for all shifters. It was a fairly new development, but the entire paranormal community seemed to have come together and unified the system a few years before he'd moved to the forest.

"I know, Vic." Kem sighed and said something muffled away from the phone. When a female voice answered him, Vic was sure that he was right about Kem being in bed.

"I need to ask a favour," Vic said, waiting nervously for Kem to respond.

"Go on," Kem replied after a moment. Vic glanced at Nita, to find her dark eyes widened and looking at him. That look gave him a feeling that he couldn't quite name, all he knew was that he wanted to make it so she always looked at him that way.

"I think I might have accidentally mated," Vic admitted sheepishly.

"What?" Kem half-shouted down the phone. "How could you do that? You know what that means, right?"

"Kem, give me the phone," the female voice demanded.

"Lia, stay out of this," Kem said, the hint of a growl behind his words. "Fine," he said with a sigh.

"Hello?" the female voice asked.

"Er, hi," Vic answered, feeling slightly weird to be talking to Kem's mate without ever being formally introduced.

"What Kem meant to say, is what happened?" she said calmly. A purring noise down the phone line told Vic that his brother had shifted, probably due to the shock. While shifter could change forms at will, it had been known for extreme emotions to cause spontaneous shifting too.

"We, er, bit each other during…" Vic let his words trail off, not wanting to discuss his sex life with anyone, much less a woman he'd never actually met.

"Sex?" Lia asked, sounding amused. "I'm mated to a shifter, Vic, I'm not exactly a prude."

"Yes, during sex," Vic said. Nita slipped her arms around his waist, and pressed her naked chest against his back. If she carried on, then he wasn't going to be able to concentrate on the conversation he was having. Not that he wanted her to stop. He rested his free hand on top of hers.

"I think it can be undone," Lia mused. Her wording had Vic worried though. If it couldn't be undone, then he'd tied Nita to him forever, and this wasn't the kind of life he wanted to enforce on anyone.

"Think?" Nita squeaked. From Lia's chuckle on the other end, the word had carried down the phone line too.

"Yes, think. It's the kind of thing that has to be sorted by the Council though," Lia replied after she'd finished laughing. Vic groaned inwardly. The last thing he wanted was to go before the Council. They'd probably have a thing or two to say about him abandoning his post.

"Any way of avoiding that?" he asked, thinking back to the shifters that had been on the Council when he'd last gone before them. He didn't know any of their names, but there'd been a lot of alpha males in the room, and it hadn't provided for a comfortable atmosphere.

"The Council has changed a lot, Vic," Kem said down the phone, having shifted back to human form at some point during the conversation. "I was in front of them a few months ago. The whole system seems to have changed. Have you heard of Arabella Reed?"

"No," Vic answered instantly, not recognising the name.

"She's really brought the Council into the twenty-first century," Kem said.

"She?" Vic was surprised; there'd never been any women on the Council while he'd been actually fulfilling his role of alpha.

"Yes, she." Kem sounded amused. Nita remained silent behind Vic, probably because she wasn't fully versed in how Shifter politics worked her. Except that as it turned out, Vic wasn't as well versed in it as he thought he was either.

"Okay, we'll go before the Council," Vic said.

"We'll make up the spare room for you," Lia said cheerfully. "Or do we need two rooms?" She sounded as if she was frowning and Vic didn't quite know how to respond.

"One room's fine," Nita said loudly enough for Lia to hear down the phone.

"Great, see you in a few days," Lia said.

"See you soon, bro," Kem added sounding smug.

CHAPTER SEVEN

Nita hung back as Vic knocked on the door of what could only be described as a mansion. The building was huge, and reminiscent of how her family had lived before they'd been killed. At first, she'd missed the space and the wealth, but she'd soon got past that. It wasn't as if she hadn't spent time outdoors and roughing it before anyway.

The door swung open, revealing a tall broad man who looked a lot like Vic, and an equally tall blonde woman, with a massive smile on her face.

"You must be Vic," she said, bouncing out the door and embracing Vic in an awkward hug. He didn't hug her back, and looked highly uncomfortable with the contact. Without thinking, Nita placed a comforting hand on Vic's back, hoping that he took the gesture the way she meant it to. The blonde woman let go and turned to Nita. "Hi, I'm Lia."

"Nita," she responded, and held out her hand. Lia took it, shaking firmly but looking like she wanted to hug Nita too.

Besides them, the two men eyed each other up, and Nita wondered which one of them would break first. Lia withdrew her hand, and watched the two men for a second.

"Kemnebi," Lia said in a stern voice. The brothers broke their stare and Kem finally smiled, making the resemblance between the two of them even stronger.

"Hi," Vic said, his voice cracking slightly. On their way to Kem and Lia's home, he'd told Nita that this was the first time he'd seen his brother in years. And that he was nervous about it.

"Vic," Kem replied.

"Want to leave them to it?" Lia whispered conspiratorially.

"Yes," Nita replied. She was a little unsure about spending time with a woman she didn't know, it was preferable to being close to the sheer volume of testosterone that the two men were giving off.

"I have wine in the kitchen. White or red?" she asked.

"Erm…" Nita had never really had a chance to drink any wine, never mind the expensive kind that she imagined Lia and Kem drank. "I've never really tried any," she admitted softly, thankful that the two men were ignoring them. Surprisingly, Lia's eyes lit up, as if she was plotting something.

"Let's change that," she grabbed Nita's hand and pulled her through the door. Nita followed quickly, looking around the beautiful house as she did. The inside was surprisingly comfortable compared to what she'd imagined when approaching the front.

In a matter of moments, the two of them arrived in a sparkling kitchen, with more gadgets and appliances than Nita could have imagined existed. She looked around, and her gaze locked onto a tree which seemed to be planted in the corner of the room. It wasn't even in a pot, but planted in the ground, with a sky light above it.

"Oh, that's my tree," Lia said when she saw where Nita was looking.

"Your tree?" Nita responded dumbly.

"I'm a dryad," Lia responded. "Well, half a dryad I guess. I can shift now too. But that's the tree I was tethered to at birth. Kem hated every second of moving it for me, he kept worrying that he'd kill it," she said, a fond smile on her face.

"What would have happened if he had?" Nita asked, curiosity getting the better of her.

"Now? Nothing. But before I mated with Kem, I'd probably have become seriously ill."

"Because of a tree?" Nita asked, shocked by how much power a tree seemed to have.

"It's a nymph thing. We can't go far from our tethers. I mean, it's flexible. Taking a blossom with me when I left the house for a few days worked for me," Lia explained, handing Nita a cold glass filled with a pale yellow liquid that she assumed must be the wine the other woman had promised.

"Thanks," she muttered, unsure about the smell. Slowly, she took a small sip, pulling a face when she tasted the tartness of the drink. Lia laughed softly.

"Not for you?" Lia asked softly. Nita shook her head.

"What can I get you instead?" she asked.

"Surprise me," Nita said, not wanting her possible sister-in-law to realise that she was as uncultured as she was. Which stopped her cold. She was still mated to Vic, which was what they were here to fix. Except that she kept forgetting that it was something that needed fixing.

"Nita, are you okay?" Lia sounded sympathetic, but Nita wasn't completely convinced. Why should this woman, who was effectively a stranger, care how she felt?

"Sorry, lost in thought for a moment."

"Nuh-uh," Lia said, moving Nita to the swing seat that was under the cherry blossom tree. On its own, the swing would have been as out of place as the tree, but together they kind of worked. "Now, what's bothering you?"

Nita debated what to tell her. Especially as she wasn't sure if she could trust the woman. At the end of the day, Lia was mated to Vic's brother, and that meant that she was likely against Nita in the whole situation. But, other than Lia, Nita had no one. And surely someone to talk to for a night was better than no one to talk to ever.

"I'm just worried about the false mating," she admitted softly.

"Are you sure it's false?" Lia asked, a curious expression on her face.

"Why wouldn't it be?" Nita asked, wondering where the other woman was going.

"Neither of you are acting like false mates," Lia said.

"If there was a way of acting like false mates, then people wouldn't accidentally mate in the first place," Nita muttered.

"Not true, people are colossally stupid; even when they pretend not to be." Nita smiled at Lia's

39

statement, realising that it was likely true. She supposed that the dryad could be right about other things too, and that maybe there was something more between her and Vic. But she didn't want to get her hopes up. That was a sure-fire way to get her heartbroken.

CHAPTER EIGHT

VIC STARED AT HIS BROTHER, not quite knowing what to do. It'd been too long since he'd last seen Kem, and it was almost like looking in a mirror. They were a similar height, and both had the lithe but muscular frames that panther shifters were known for; though Vic had a slightly stockier frame. Partly due to him technically being the panther alpha, and partly due to his life in the woods.

To his surprise, Kem pulled Vic towards him, and slapped Vic on the back in a bear hug. Even thinking the word distracted him with thoughts of Nita and where she might have gone when his brother's mate had dragged her off.

Finally, Vic hugged his brother back. If he was honest, he was surprised that Kem hadn't punched him; it's what he would have done. For the first time since their parents' deaths, shame washed through Vic. He hadn't thought about the fact he'd basically abandoned his younger brother and his people while he dealt with his grief. And now that it had hit him, he couldn't ignore it.

"I'm sorry," he said, his voice cracking. He was just thankful that Nita wasn't about to witness his loss of masculinity; she'd never want him then.

"It's fine," Kem said, his voice shaking almost as much as Vic's was.

"You never were good at lying," Vic responded, half laughing despite himself and reminding him of happier times. While they had their own interests and lives, the two brothers had been close growing up, and it was that more than anything that Vic regretted losing the most.

Kem pulled back, an indiscernible expression on his face. Vic didn't want to think too much about it, especially as it probably touched on Vic's choice to abandon him.

"Lia seems nice," he ventured in an attempt to distract Kem from whatever he was thinking. To Vic's surprise, it actually worked, and Kem's face softened instantly.

"That's an understatement." Kem sighed, and oddly, jealousy gripped onto Vic's heart. He'd never really thought about a mate until recently, but it seemed like at least a part of him wanted what his brother had.

"Tell me about her," he prompted.

"She's my world, Vic. I hope you'll find someone like that to you one day," Kem said.

Vic glanced back towards the house they were still standing outside, before looking away quickly. Getting his hopes up about Nita wasn't going to help matters. He could feel himself getting too attached already, and that was only going to end badly when they ended their accidental mating.

"Are you staying after you've been before the Council?" Kem asked cautiously.

"I don't know," Vic answered, his thoughts still on the woman inside Kem's house.

"You should; things are different now."

"But I'm different too," Vic countered, knowing that it wasn't likely to sway his brother anyway.

"True. But that's not necessarily a bad thing," Kem countered. "Is there anything I can do to convince you?" he asked, and Vic shook his head.

"No. Though there is something you can help me do while I'm here." Kem gave Vic a curious expression, and Vic steeled himself for what he had to say next. "I need help finding Nita's cousin. She's looking for him." Kem nodded thoughtfully, but didn't say anything for a moment.

"Do we have anything to go on?"

"He's likely a bear shifter, unless she comes from a mixed family. But that seems unlikely," Vic said.

"True, though it's getting more likely. Me and Lia aren't the only mated pair to break the norm recently," Kem said with a smile. It was an interesting thought, and not one that would likely sit well with a lot of shifters. But at least change was happening.

"His surname's Hendricks," Vic said with a snap of his fingers as he remembered what Nita had said when talking about her cousin.

In front of him, Kem burst out laughing, causing confusion to well up inside Vic.

"What?" he asked his brother, not quite sure what had set him off.

"Oh you'll see," Kem said through his laughter.

CHAPTER NINE

Nɪᴛᴀ ᴡᴀɪᴛᴇᴅ ɴᴇʀᴠᴏᴜsʟʏ while glancing at the door every few seconds. Lia had asked if she wanted a room of her own rather than sharing with Vic, but the mere idea of that had made Nita uncomfortable.

What hadn't though, was a hot shower, and for the first time in weeks, Nita felt truly clean. She ran her hand through her dark hair, enjoying how silky and smooth it felt. She missed feeling like this more than she'd realised while out in the woods.

The door creaked, and she looked up, anxious to see Vic again, even if it had only been an hour or two. She'd been talking with Lia, and had found herself surprisingly at ease around the woman, almost to the point of feeling like she was family. Which she kind of guessed they were at the moment.

He stepped into the room, looking a little worse

for wear, and Nita worried her hands together in order to stop herself from reaching out for him.

"Nita?" His question came with a hint of surprise. Like he hadn't expected her to be in here. She bit her lip, hoping that she hadn't overstepped the boundaries.

"Sorry, when Lia asked..." She started, only to be cut off by Vic striding forward and capturing her lips with his.

The kiss was rough, and almost desperate. Like he was trying to tell her something with it that he daren't speak aloud. Nita mewled into the kiss, surprised at herself for making a noise like that, but she pressed her body into his all the same.

A large, coarse hand slipped between the fabric of the robe Nita had borrowed, making its way across her bare skin. Vic growled, breaking their kiss so that he could nip along Nita's jaw.

She leaned her head back, allowing him better access the soft skin of her throat, and the stubble on his jaw only added to the sensation.

"Nita," he groaned against her neck, slipping the robe down her shoulders and leaving her naked in front of him.

"Vic," she whispered, feeling more vulnerable now than when she'd been naked with him before.

Something between them had changed, though she wasn't sure what it was; only that it wasn't their accidental mating. "You're wearing too many clothes," she said. He chuckled, and took a step backwards.

Hands on his shirt, he stopped for a moment to look at her, the hungry look in his eyes telling Nita that she'd made the right decision in what room she stayed in.

He whipped his shirt over his head, revealing every inch of his muscled torso. Before she could do anything about it, like reach out and touch, he unbuttoned his jeans and pushed them to the floor. Glancing down, she licked her lips as she took in the sight that confirmed her earlier thought; this was the right room.

To Nita's surprise, Vic picked her up, and almost threw her down onto the bed. She looked up at him, and saw the same desire she was feeling reflected back at her in his eyes. Vic leaned over her, and not wanting to wait, Nita reached out her hand and drew him to her with a firm press to the back of his neck.

Vic came willingly, caging her with his arms as he kissed her back fiercely. She bucked against him, desperate for the two of them to move even closer together, and to feel the delicious slide of skin on skin that wasn't like anything she'd experienced with any other man ever.

She reached down between them and took him firmly in her hand, stroking slowly and smiling into their kiss as she felt his breath hitch. He moved one of his arms, and she felt his fingers trailing across her skin and between her legs. Slowly, he pushed his fingers into her and she arched upwards, pushing their bodies together and breaking their kiss.

She moved her hand faster, causing Vic to do the same, both of them panting heavily. Nita could feel the pleasure building up inside her, but something still wasn't right.

"Please, Vic. Now," she said through her pants. He withdrew his fingers, causing an involuntary whimper at the loss, but he made up for it by removing her hand from around him, and getting himself into position.

Their eyes locked as he began to move inside her. Something passed between them, though Nita couldn't think straight enough to even begin to figure out what; thinking would just have to wait.

She moved against him, falling into the natural rhythm of their bodies as they came together, not as hurried as the first time, and definitely something more. Pleasure began to build again, and she knew that, despite their slow pace, she wasn't going to be able to last much longer.

Nita dug her nails into Vic's back, not caring if she drew blood or not as all thoughts raced out of her head. To her, there was nothing more than this moment. Nothing but the connection between the two of them. And while the urge to bite wasn't there, she recognised the feeling from when it had been.

Nita shuddered and cried out as pleasure exploded behind her eyelids, her body taking on a mind of its own until she was spent.

"Nita," Vic groaned against her skin as he joined her. He collapsed onto the bed beside her, their limbs still entwined and their bodies slick with sweat. But Nita couldn't recall any time at all when she'd felt as content as this. She just hoped that it would last.

CHAPTER TEN

Vic fidgeted with his belt loop as he looked up at the opulent Council building in front of him. It'd been so long since he'd been in front of the Shifter Council, that he was worried how they'd take it. Kem had told him that most of the members had changed, but that really wasn't helping.

A soft hand landed on his, and untangled his fingers from the belt loop. The touch was reassuring in a way he hadn't thought possible, and he looked to the left, pleased to see that it was Nita standing next to him. Her dark hair shined in the sunlight, and a caring expression was in her eyes. He didn't know who else's hand he'd thought it would be, but something in him was glad that it was hers. Even if he wasn't quite ready to admit that out loud yet.

"You'll be fine," she whispered softly. In front of

them, Kem and Lia were having their own mumbled conversation, possibly about what they thought was going to happen once they were in the Council chambers.

"That's easy to say," Vic muttered.

"You didn't do anything wrong," she soothed, squeezing his hand gently.

"I abandoned my people, Nita. It's not going to be easy in there," he reminded her, grimacing as he thought about how he'd react in the Council's place.

"Because you were mourning. It's hardly fair to expect you to carry on as if nothing had happened," she half-whispered, half-shouted. Her cheeks were flushed, as if she was taking it as a personal affront. Wanting to calm her, Vic slipped an arm around her waist and pulled her to him.

They reached the Council door, and Kem knocked a couple of times, waiting with a small smile on his face. Which confused Vic. Going to see the Council wasn't something to smile about.

The door swung open, and a petite auburn-haired woman stood in the frame.

"Kemnebi," she said with a slight hint of amusement in her voice.

"Arabella," he replied, equally as amused. "How's Bjorn?"

"Well, thank you," the woman replied, her face

lighting up. She opened the door further, and the four of them trailed in. Arabella gave Vic an odd look as he walked past her, yet more strange behaviour. This was nothing like the Council meetings he remembered.

"Are we ready yet?" a man drawled from one of the Council chairs. Vic looked towards the voice, but was surprised to find the chair in shadow. Nearby, the woman muttered something that sounded like she was cursing the man's name, but Vic didn't want to ask.

To his surprise, Arabella made her way to the only vacant Council seat, and plopped herself down in it, glaring in the direction of the man's voice. Looking around the room at the other three Council members, Vic was surprised to see that two of them were also women; another change since he'd last been here.

"I thought we'd got rid of you Kemnebi?" a blonde man joked from between an even blonder woman, and one with chocolate brown hair; like he was framed with complete opposites.

"You are," Kem said through a smile, then paused dramatically. Beside him, Lia sighed loudly, before taking a step forward.

"This is Kem's brother, Vic," she said when Kem stayed silent.

"The deserter?" the man from the end almost hissed the word as he leaned forward in his chair, the light finally hitting his face. Vic was surprised to find that he was almost classically handsome, not to mention younger than he'd expected.

"Drayce," Arabella admonished, and to Vic's surprise, the man relaxed back into his chair. "Are you back to take up your position again?"

Vic tried to start saying "no" but stopped before he could. Something just wouldn't let him say the word. Glancing to the side, he suspected that there was a simple explanation.

"Something more important," he said instead. Arabella quirked an eyebrow in response, but didn't say anything. As if she knew that she'd break him with her silence. And it worked. "I need your help finding someone. Nita's lost her family, but she has a cousin still living around here we think," he said.

"Do we have a name?" Arabella asked. From where he was standing, Vic could see Kem sniggering, though he didn't know why. Or at least, he was sniggering until Lia batted his arm and gave him a warning look.

"Hendricks," Nita said, speaking up for the first time. The blonde man started to laugh, while Arabella smothered a smile with her hand, attempting to look sternly at Kem.

"You couldn't have just phoned?" she asked.

"And missed this?" The blonde man chuckled.

"Do I need to get Rory here, Alden?" Arabella snapped, and the man stopped laughing, though Vic could still see the man's shoulders shaking.

"What's going on?" Vic asked, pulling Nita closer to him so that she was protected.

"I'm Arabella Hendricks," the auburn-haired woman said.

"But my cousin's male," Nita said, confusion sounding in her voice.

"Yes. I imagine he's my mate," Arabella said, leaving Vic floored. Of all the revelations he'd expected, that wasn't one he'd imagined.

CHAPTER ELEVEN

Nita didn't have the words to describe how she was feeling at this moment in time. She supposed that she should be elated at the prospect of meeting her one remaining family member. Instead, she was feeling sick to her stomach.

A warm hand rested on her back, and she took a deep breath, enjoying the scent she'd come to recognise as completely Vic. And to say he thought that they weren't properly mated, it was a scent that made her feel safer than she ever had before. Maybe Lia was on to something when she questioned if the false mating was really all that false.

"Nita, it'll be fine," Vic said in her ear and she leaned back into him.

"What if he doesn't like me?"

"Why wouldn't he?" Vic asked, frowning down at

her as if he genuinely couldn't understand the concept.

"He doesn't know me," she reminded him.

"Give him ten minutes in your company and he'll know you," Vic said with a tender expression on his face. He leaned down and tucked a stray piece of hair behind her ear. Yet more evidence that their mating was more than it seemed. Nita pulled a face, not quite believing him.

"Yeah, right," she muttered.

Vic moved around so that he was facing her properly; an intense look in his eyes. They stood there for a few moments, not moving or saying a word as something passed between them that Nita couldn't name.

"Yes, I'm right. We're going to go in there, talk to your cousin, and then you'll see," he said earnestly.

"What if he isn't nice?" she asked in a small voice that she was sure betrayed her true insecurities. It was one thing if her only family didn't like her, quite another if it turned out that she didn't like them.

"I doubt Kem would have let us come if your cousin wasn't a good man. Plus, you already met his wife," Vic reminded her.

"True," Nita conceded, not liking that he was right. It could end up setting a dangerous precedent.

"Now, are you ready?" he asked, and Nita nodded.

"I guess," she replied. Vic gestured towards the intercom on the building of flats, and nervously, Nita pressed the button.

CHAPTER TWELVE

Vic wasn't sure what to expect from the upcoming meeting, though he wasn't surprised when the red-headed shifter from the Council opened the door of the flat.

"Hi," she said brightly, opening the door fully and waving them through. Everything about the home they entered was contrary to Vic's. The décor was modern, with sharp whites and bold colours. Nothing like his rustic cabin. He glanced sideways at Nita, who moved closer to him, as if she too was feeling slightly overwhelmed by the contrast in surroundings.

The two of them were led into a room, where a broad dark-haired man was sat on a sofa, looking particularly uncomfortable. Accessing him quickly, Vic decided that the man wasn't a threat, and took his attention back to Nita, who'd stopped dead in the doorway.

"Is everything okay?" the woman who'd answered the door said. Vic could tell that she was genuinely concerned, though whether it was because of Nita's discomfort, or the man's, Vic wasn't sure. "Can I get anyone anything? Tea? Coffee? Water? Wine?" she asked quickly, the nervousness obviously catching.

"Ari," the man on the sofa said, his voice both a plea and a comfort. Vic watched them exchange glances, jealousy rearing up for a moment. Without thinking about it, he reached backwards until his hand made contact with Nita's. She squeezed his hand, and stepped closer to him, at which point, Vic wrapped his arm around her waist.

"You look just like him," Nita said, and the two other shifters turned to look at her. Vic wanted more than anything to stand in front of her and keep her safe from their prying eyes, but knew that this wasn't the right situation to do that in.

"Grandfather?" the man asked softly.

"Yes," she replied. Across the room, Ari relaxed visibly and Vic smiled to himself. He imagined that Ari had been feeling as protective over her mate as he was over his. He tried to remind himself that Nita wasn't actually his real mate, but something in his head was blocking the idea, and try as he might, he just couldn't accept that what was between them wasn't real. "I'm Nita," she added.

"Bjorn," he replied, a thoughtful look on his face. "I remember you." Next to Vic, Nita frowned.

"I'm sorry, I don't remember you," she said, sounding disappointed. Vic gave her waist a quick squeeze, trying to convey that he was there to support her. The weak smile she gave him showed that it had worked, though maybe not as well as he'd intended.

"You were only a baby at the time. Aunt Martha had brought you to visit us. I was a spoilt brat of five, so didn't have much time for you," Bjorn said, a sad look passing over his face. "I'm sorry for that now."

"Why? It's not like it would have changed anything?" Nita blurted out.

"No, but maybe it would have meant that we'd have been closer. Then neither of us would have been alone for so long," he said. As far as Vic could tell, the man was being genuinely sincere, which filled him with hope regarding Nita staying around here.

"Maybe," Nita said with a sigh. "But you have Ari now, and I…" she trailed off, and Vic wondered what she was about to say. Unfortunately, Nita didn't seem inclined to carry on with what she was saying.

"Have me," Vic said, surprising himself. He hadn't

meant to voice the thought aloud, but the look he got from Nita made it all worth it.

Ari moved over to her mate's side and sat on the arm of the sofa, rubbing Bjorn's back in a way that was both affectionate and slightly possessive.

"This is Vic, Kemnebi's brother," she said.

"Oh?" Bjorn sounded surprised, and Vic didn't blame him. Everyone on the Shifter Council would know that Vic had been missing in action for the past few years. They'd probably had conversations about how to deal with him being missing and everything. "And you're back now?" Bjorn asked, his tone ever so slightly accusatory.

"Yes," Vic responded.

"He's helped me a lot, Bjorn," Nita added, her eyes flaring with a protective vibe.

"Hmmm," Bjorn said.

"I'm back," Vic said, steeling his tone. He didn't want anyone to think he was going to flake again. He had someone he wanted to stay around for this time.

"That's good to hear," Ari said, her tone shifting slightly to the same one she used in the Council chamber. If he had to guess, Vic would say that it was her authoritative voice, and from the look on Bjorn's face, it wasn't always unwelcome when she used it.

"But this isn't about me, this is about Bjorn and Nita," Vic said.

"Very well," Ari said amused. "Nita, what are your plans now?" she asked, softening her voice when she talked to Vic's mate.

"I don't know. I've never really had a steady place to base myself, so..." she trailed off, looking embarrassed.

"We can help you find something," Vic said softly, while Ari looked on thoughtfully.

"What kind of thing do you want to do? I mean job wise?" the other woman asked. Nita looked thoughtful.

"I've never really given it much thought. I'd only just finished high school when things happened. Jobs didn't really seem like a big deal after that," she finished lamely, and Vic longed to pull her more into his arms, but didn't dare considering they were still stood in the other couple's living room. He didn't think Nita's cousin would appreciate what he'd do to her then.

"Why don't we have lunch tomorrow? We can talk about some options if you want?" Ari asked.

"Thank you," Nita said. "I'd like that." She smiled at the woman.

CHAPTER THIRTEEN

NITA HADN'T HAD a female friend before. And now, as she watched her new cousin-in-law approach, she'd already caught herself envying Arabella; the woman seemed to have it all. Friends, a loving mate and a successful career. Though Nita supposed that at least she had one of those things. Except that she didn't. Vic wasn't her mate, she had to try and remember that.

"Hi, sorry I'm late," she said, taking a seat opposite Nita.

"It's no problem, Arabella," Nita replied with a weak smile.

"My friends call me Ari," the other woman responded kindly, brushing down her suit skirt as she did. "Just came from work," she added needlessly. It was the middle of the week, and it wasn't like the other shifters had known she was coming.

"What exactly is it that you do?" Nita asked, genuinely curious. She'd gathered that Ari was a lawyer from what she'd heard other say, but that didn't really mean much to her.

"I keep innocent people from going to prison," she replied instantly, a broad smile on her face.

"Do you get a lot of innocent clients?" Nita asked, cocking her head. She'd have thought that most people needing a lawyer to keep them out of prison had generally done the deed.

"More than you'd think. It's normally people being blamed for something one of ours has done," Ari said quietly. Nita glanced around to make sure that no one was listening. Unsurprisingly, they weren't. The restaurant was busy and full of chatter despite it being a Tuesday.

"That's a problem?" Nita said, aghast at the thought. Where their family came from, paranormals kept to themselves and there was more of an issue with humans hunting shifters in the forests than there was paranormals going off the rails. Ari nodded, and took a sip of the water that a waiter had poured before she'd even arrived.

"In a big city like this, you bet it is. Just a couple of months ago we uncovered a necromancer who was off the rails," Ari said, waving over one of the waiting staff.

"Hi, what can I get for you?" the blonde waitress asked.

"I'll have the belly pork, please," Ari said without even looking at the menu. The waitress turned to Nita.

"The salmon, please," she said. She'd studied the options in minute detail while waiting for Ari to arrive, and had been shocked by the variety. She hadn't been in many restaurants since she was a child, she'd never had the money to, and certainly not one as fancy as this one.

"Anything else?" the waitress asked, smiling politely.

"No thank you," Ari told her. The other woman walked away to complete their order, and Nita let out a breath that she hadn't realised she was holding. Having a conversation like the two of them just had was dangerous, she could appreciate that. But she was also too curious to let it drop.

"So, what happened to the necromancer?" Nita asked.

"He's on trial with the High Council now. One of the Shifter Council and his mate managed to catch him," Ari said, smiling to herself in satisfaction.

"And that's it? No harm done?" Nita asked curiously.

"Well, the Necromancer Council's been disbanded, and they're in complete disarray, but other than that it doesn't seem so."

"When you say his mate, is she another shifter?" Nita asked what she'd really wanted to, rather than what she felt she should. Ari looked at her with a knowing look in her eye.

"No, she's a necromancer. Why do you ask?"

"I was just wondering if different kinds of shifters could mate," she admitted. She wasn't sure that she should, but Nita figured that she may as well. At best, she'd form a stronger bond with Ari, and maybe make her first friend in years. At worst, well she guessed she never actually had to see the woman again once her bond to Vic was broken.

"I hope so," Ari said, giggling slightly. Nita just waited for her to continue. "I'm not a bear," she added finally, and Nita's eyes widened.

"So..."

"So, they're perfectly normal. Well, maybe not normal. But they're becoming more commonplace. I hardly think that Bjorn and I are the only ones. I mean, there's you and Vic for a start," she said.

"Me and Vic aren't..."

"Oh, please," Ari interrupted. "It's obvious to

anyone with eyes that there's a connection between you and Vic. You just haven't accepted it yet."

Nita felt herself smiling, but couldn't stop it.

"Or you do accept it, you're just too scared to talk to each other about it," Ari said triumphantly.

"How do I know for real though?" Nita asked. She might be worrying unnecessarily, but she'd never even thought she was in love before, so the whole mating thing was completely new to her.

"The sex is the best you've ever had," Ari dead-panned and Nita's jaw dropped. Not because what Ari said wasn't true, it was, but more the matter of fact way that she said it.

"That's it?" Nita asked, sceptical that it was that simple.

"Well no," Ari admitted, laughing slightly. "You'll feel it in yourself. You'll want to be with him at every opportunity. You'll find yourself thinking about things like babies, even when you never had before." Ari smiled to herself, making Nita think that there was something more personal about that last one.

"Oh."

"The look on your face says that all that's true," Ari said.

"I think it might be. You're not the first person to say it."

"Let's guess, Lia?"

"Yes," Nita said.

"Kemnebi really married up with that one," Ari said.

"I'd hope so, she's a scientist after all," Nita added. Feeling that the subject of mates was done, and making a mental note that she'd need to talk to Vic about it as soon as she saw him again. It was probably time that they accepted what was between them.

Their food arrived, and Nita had to admit that it was quite possibly the best fish she'd ever eaten. Maybe now that she'd have a place to properly call home, she could learn to cook in ways that didn't involve an open fire.

CHAPTER FOURTEEN

VIC PACED BACK and forth as he waited for Nita to return from lunch with Ari. He was worried about her, and he couldn't quite explain why. She was a grown woman and perfectly capable of looking after herself. Especially considering that she could turn into a bear at will.

To his surprise, Nita bounced down the path towards Kem's front door, looking considerably lighter than she had before she'd left.

"I take it everything went well?" he asked, receiving a wide smile in return.

"Very." She bounced up to him and threw her arms around his neck. Without thinking, he leaned down and captured her lips in a searing kiss. How he'd ever thought that the mating between them was fake was beyond him, but he now knew that he never wanted to let her go.

Nita made a slight mewling sound as they kissed, only spurring him on more. He slipped his arm around her waist and held her tight to him, no longer caring who saw them.

"Ahem," a male voice interrupted, causing Nita to break their kiss.

"Go away Kem," she muttered, causing Vic's brother to laugh and a low chuckle to escape him too. She was definitely in a better place than she had been.

"How's Arabella?" Kem asked, ignoring Nita's dismissal.

"She's fine, now go away," she said, turning her head so that she could glare at Kem, though thankfully not leaving Vic's arms. He wasn't sure that he could stand the thought of her leaving him right now.

"You might want to take this inside before one of you gets your teeth out," Kem said, still chuckling to himself as if it was something particularly amusing rather than an intense moment between Vic and his mate.

"He may have a point," Vic said as Nita pouted at him. He nuzzled his nose into her hair, bringing his lips up so that they were level with her ear. "Inside we have a bed," he reminded her. Nita jumped out of his hold and grabbed his hand, pulling him through the front door and away from Vic's clearly amused brother.

She dragged him down the corridor, and straight into their room. Nita pushed him onto the bed, and Vic went willingly, seating himself so that she could easily straddle his lap. Luckily for him, she obliged, her legs stretching out on either side of his waist.

She captured his lips with hers, deepening the kiss almost as soon as it had started. He kissed her back, loving how passionate she was, and how the kiss did more for him than any he'd ever experienced before. After a few moments, he broke the kiss, regretting it almost instantly.

"Nita," he half-groaned.

"Hmm," she responded, sounding almost sleepy.

"We need to talk." That stopped her, and she slid off his lap to sit next to him. Instantly, Vic felt her loss and longed to pull her back into his arms.

"That doesn't sound good," she said, a sad note in her voice.

"It's not bad," he reasoned. They sat there in silence, neither one of them wanting to be the one that started the conversation. Though in Nita's defence, she had no idea what it was he wanted to say. Which meant that he was the one that had to start this. Taking a steadying breath, he said what he had to. "I'm your mate."

"Yes, I know. You bit me," Nita said evenly.

"No, I'm your proper mate," he said, thinking that she hadn't quite understood what he meant.

"Yes, I know. Lia and Ari told me."

"They did?" he asked, surprised. Maybe because he'd expected Nita to be a little more freaked out than she was.

"Yes. Apparently, it was something about the way that we've been looking at each other. Plus, the whole mating bond thing we thought we did by accident." She shrugged, like it wasn't a big deal.

"Kem said the same," he admitted quietly.

"Then maybe we need to start listening to them." She took his hand in hers and gave it a squeeze, before letting go to draw patterns on the back of it. He was surprised to find that the trace of her fingertips against his skin made it tingle, but then, if everyone else was to be believed, including his inner panther, then she was his mate, and that was how she should be making him feel.

"And you're okay with this?" he asked her.

"Vic, I've been alone for too long. Why wouldn't I be okay with this? I get you, I get your family, and I've even found my own. Meeting you was the best thing that ever happened to me. Being mated to you is hardly going to be a chore," she said, her eyes glittering with a mix of emotions, and Vic was pleased to see that sadness wasn't one of them. Instead, she looked content. Like he really had managed to lift a weight from her shoulders.

"You've done all that for me too," he said.

"No, I haven't. You'd have come back in your own time," she said with an earnestness that he wanted to believe, but wasn't sure that he could.

"I don't think I would have," he admitted. If left to his own devices, he'd likely have stayed in the woods for the rest of his life. Even if Kem had had the foresight to come and get him.

"I've seen you with Kem and the others, I don't believe that's true."

"Hmm," he said noncommittally. He still wasn't convinced.

"Are you going to take up the alpha position again?" she asked.

"I'm not sure. It's well within everyone's rights not to let me." Plus, he wasn't sure how they'd take him being mated to a bear shifter. They might be okay with it, especially given Kem and Lia's relationship and their position in society, but then they might not be. The alpha was supposed to be a symbol of strength and their people. Having mixed cubs would confuse the line of succession as well, which was never going to end well.

"Whatever happens, I'm with Vic Davis," she said, adoration shining in her face. "Now, where were we?" The adoration changed into something much more wicked, and Vic soon found himself flat on his back, with his beautiful mate perched above him, her long dark hair falling down to shelter their faces.

NITA WATCHED on as Vic began to take charge of the young shifters who were learning to hunt. He'd been right about the panthers not wanting to accept him as the alpha any more, but he'd also been surprisingly calm about it. In fact, he'd almost been happy. At first, it had worried her, but it soon became clear that he was happier away from the politics of the shifter world. At least they still got to attend the balls and parties though. It turned out that Nita loved to dress up nice, probably because she'd never really had the chance before.

"He's really changed," Lia said from beside Nita.

"No, he hasn't. He's just more himself," Nita replied without looking away from where her mate was. She touched her stomach lightly, finding herself longing for a child of her own. Seeing him with the younger shifters was making her broody, especially as she could see what a good father he'd be one day.

"Something you need to tell me?" Lia asked. Nita turned to her sister-in-law and as greeted with a smirk.

"No." She sighed. She'd never thought about children this much before. Lia raised an eyebrow.

"If you want one, he'd have one in a heartbeat," Lia said.

"I'm not so sure," Nita said, looking back towards Vic and the young shifters.

"Really? Because he keeps looking at you, then at the cubs and back again. I'd say he wants one as badly as you do. Maybe even more," Lia said. Nita stood in silence, contemplating what Lia had said.

After a few moments, Lia wandered off; to do what, Nita wasn't sure. Kem wasn't about, he was too busy doing the Alpha duties he'd taken on properly now that Vic had officially stood down. As much as she loved her sister-in-law, Nita didn't mind being left alone. Not when she had so much to be thinking about anyway.

"Alright, go get some lunch," Vic's voice boomed through the small clearing, and the children with him ran off towards the picnic benches where food had been laid out for them. Vic spotted Nita watching him, and waved. Her heart skipped a beat as he slowly prowled towards her. They may have been together for a while now, but he still seemed to have that effect on her; she hoped he always would.

"You're amazing with them," she said as he reached her.

"Thank you," he replied, before dropping a quick kiss on her lips. She wanted to take it deeper, but now really wasn't the time.

"Have a baby with me," she blurted out. Her hand flew to her mouth, and her eyes widened in horror that she'd just said that aloud. But Vic didn't look surprised. In fact, a wide smile spread over his face.

"Any time," he said, his eyes twinkling.

"Really?"

"Really," he replied. He slipped his arms around her waist and pulled her to him, kissing her deeply this time despite where they were. But she supposed, given the circumstances, it was acceptable.

The End

Thank you for reading *The Bear's Claws*! If you want more paranormal romance, why not check out *The Familiar's Wings:* http://books2read.com/thefamiliarswings

EXCERPT: THE FAMILIAR'S WINGS

Read on for an excerpt from The Familiar's Wings, the next book in The Paranormal Council: http:// books2read.com/thefamiliarswings

* * *

ELIZA WALKED THROUGH THE DOOR, grateful to be home after a horrendous day at work. She'd graduated from university the year before, and had been lucky enough to get an entry level marketing job for a well-known clothing brand. And she hated it. A lot of her job was tedious, but she hadn't known what she wanted to do when she finished her degree, so had settled on what she was best at.

She waved her hand towards the kitchen, a bright blue spark leaving her fingertips, animating a chopping board and knife. The day her Mum had taught her to use her magic for cooking, had been one of the best of her life. Before that, she'd been made to cook by hand, which just made using magic all the better. She'd known she was a witch since she was a little girl, but her powers hadn't manifested until she reached eighteen. For some reason, witches either developed magic while they were still toddlers, or when they reached adulthood. At first, Eliza had resented being one of the late bloomers, but seeing the havoc her younger sister, Camille, had caused, she'd finally decided that it was a blessing in disguise.

A chirping noise came from behind her, and a small smile crossed Eliza's face.

"Hey, Bluebird," she crooned at her familiar. All witches had one, though very few would ever be seen by other people. Bluebird had appeared to her after she'd been left alone on her eighteenth birthday, thankfully after she'd got a basic grip on her new powers. Much like Eliza's normal magic, Bluebird was made of blue sparks, and yet, she didn't seem to be controllable in the same way. Bluebird appeared when she wanted to, and did what she wanted to, making her more like a low maintenance pet than magic.

Eliza poured herself a glass of white wine, having

learnt from experience that there were a few things that magic couldn't, and shouldn't, take care of. There'd been too many liquid related accidents for her to trust her powers with pouring.

Eliza jumped at the sound of her phone ringing, and she made the mistake of answering before checking who it was; not that it would really matter. The only people who were likely to call her were her parents, or her eighteen-year-old sister.

"Hello," she said, taking a sip of wine.

"Hi Liz," a deep male voice sounded at the end of the line.

"Todd," she greeted. Eliza sighed inwardly, dreading the conversation to come. She wouldn't deny that she'd been attracted to Todd the first time they'd met. He was tall, dark and handsome personified, and just her type. It'd been her type ever since her first boyfriend in high school. It didn't hurt that he had one of those deep and sexy as sin voices either.

The only problem with Todd was that she'd become bored. It seemed to happen a lot with the men she dated, not that there had been many of them. At first, she'd be totally into them, especially if they reminded her of Ethan. Unfortunately, that soon seemed to wear off. Often even before they had sex.

"You free tomorrow night?" he asked.

"I'm not sure, I'll have to check." She cringed at the fact she hadn't just told him no, but she hated telling men she wasn't interested. A quick glance at her dinner told her it was almost time to put it in the oven; another job that she'd discovered was better done without magic. Unfortunately, the distraction didn't take long enough for Eliza's liking.

"Well?" Or it took too long, according to Todd.

"I'm sorry Todd, I promised Camille I'd go ice skating with her." She crossed her fingers, hoping that he wouldn't be able to sense a lie. Really, she shouldn't be worrying about that, but it was habit from growing up in a paranormal household.

A lot of paranormals were able to sense lies, especially if they were told by someone close to them. Which meant that she was probably safe from plain old human Todd.

"Seriously? Can't you cancel?" The whine in his voice made Eliza grit her teeth. He was fast becoming as annoying as he was boring. It was definitely time for her to get rid of him for good. Heartless though that may be.

"No, I can't. Bye, Todd." She hung up without waiting for a reply, and hoped that he got the message. They'd only been on three dates, which two more than Eliza should have gone on. She'd known that he wasn't the one for her after the first date. Though why she'd ever thought that was the case was beyond her. She was a witch. Her 'one' was most likely a paranormal being of some kind.

Sadness flowed through her, just like it did every other time she thought about her 'one'. Somehow, she'd got through her string of boring men without losing her romantic streak, and there was still a part of her that mourned the loss of her high school boyfriend. But like the others, Ethan had been just human, and her family moving away had been a blessing in disguise.

She'd been the one to break it off between them, and she'd done so with tears streaming down her face and her heartbreaking. She'd loved him then, and it had been difficult to do, even if her Mum had tried to persuade her that she'd get over the adolescent infatuation with time. Eliza wasn't convinced. There was still a part of her that loved him, and probably always would. After all, there was a reason that all the men since Ethan looked just like him.

She tried to change the direction of her thoughts, otherwise she'd just end up feeling worse when she remembered that she'd never see him ever again. Or that Ethan had just been human, and that there wouldn't have been any future for them anyway. It always hurt to think about that, and she suspected that she'd never truly get over him. Whatever that meant for her future. Maybe she was one of those people that would end up alone forever. She probably deserved it after what she'd done to him.

Get The Familiar's Wings here: http://books2read.com/thefamiliarswings

Books in the Paranormal Council Universe

- The Paranormal Council Series (shifter romance, completed series)
- The Fae Queen Of Winter Trilogy (paranormal/fantasy)
- Spring Fae Duology (paranormal/fantasy)
- Thornheart Coven Series (witch romance)
- Return Of The Fae Series (paranormal post-apocalyptic, completed series)
- Paranormal Criminal Investigations Series (urban fantasy mystery)
- MatchMater Paranormal Dating App Series (paranormal romance, completed series)
- The Necromancer Council Trilogy (urban fantasy)
- Standalone Stories From the Paranormal Council Universe

Books in the Obscure World

- Ashryn Barker Trilogy (urban fantasy,

completed series)

- Grimalkin Academy: Kittens Series (paranormal academy, completed series)
- Grimalkin Academy: Catacombs Trilogy (paranormal academy, completed series)
- City Of Blood Trilogy (urban fantasy)
- Grimalkin Academy: Stakes Trilogy (paranormal academy)
- The Harpy Bounty Hunter Trilogy (urban fantasy)
- Bite Of The Past (paranormal romance)
- Sabre Woods Academy (paranormal academy)
- The Shadow Seer Association (urban fantasy)

Books in the Forgotten Gods World

- The Queen of Gods Trilogy (paranormal/mythology romance)
- Forgotten Gods Series (paranormal/mythology romance, completed series)

The Grimm World

- Grimm Academy Series (fairy tale

academy)
- Fate Of The Crown Duology (Arthurian Academy)
- Once Upon An Academy Series (Fairy Tale Academy)

Other Series

- Untold Tales Series (urban fantasy fairy tales)
- The Dragon Duels Trilogy (urban fantasy dystopia)
- ME Contemporary Standalones (contemporary romance)
- Standalones
- Seven Wardens, co-written with Skye MacKinnon (paranormal/fantasy romance, completed series)
- The Firehouse Feline, co-written with Lacey Carter Andersen & L.A. Boruff (paranormal/urban fantasy romance)
- Kingdom Of Fairytales Snow White, co-written with J.A. Armitage (fantasy fairy tale)

Twin Souls Universe

- Twin Souls Trilogy, co-written with Arizona Tape (paranormal romance, completed series)
- Dragon Soul Series, co-written with Arizona Tape (paranormal romance, completed series)
- The Renegade Dragons Trilogy, co-written with Arizona Tape (paranormal romance, completed series)
- The Vampire Detective Trilogy, co-written with Arizona Tape (urban fantasy mystery, completed series)
- Amethyst's Wand Shop Mysteries Series, co-written with Arizona Tape (urban fantasy)

Mountain Shifters Universe

- Valentine Pride Trilogy, co-written with L.A. Boruff (paranormal shifter romance, completed series)
- Magic and Metaphysics Academy Trilogy, co-written with L.A. Boruff (paranormal academy, completed series)
- Mountain Shifters Standalones, co-written with L.A. Boruff (paranormal romance)

Audiobooks: www.authorlauragreenwood.co.
uk/p/audio.html

ABOUT THE AUTHOR

Laura is a USA Today Bestselling Author of paranormal and fantasy romance. When she's not writing, she can be found drinking ridiculous amounts of tea, trying to resist French Macaroons, and watching the Pitch Perfect trilogy for the hundredth time (at least!)

FOLLOW THE AUTHOR

Website: www.authorlauragreenwood.co.uk

Mailing List: www.authorlauragreenwood.co.uk/p/mailing-list-sign-up.html

Facebook Group: http://facebook.com/groups/theparanormalcouncil

Facebook Page: http://facebook.com/authorlauragreenwood

Bookbub: www.bookbub.com/authors/laura-greenwood

Instagram: www.instagram.com/authorlauragreenwood

Twitter: www.twitter.com/lauramg_tdir

Printed in Great Britain
by Amazon